ILLUSIVE SOBRIETY

ILLUSIVE SOBRIETY

The Six Disciplines Of Sobriety

Marvin Sprouse

Copyright © 2022 by Marvin Sprouse.

All rights reserved. No part of this book may be reproduced in any form or by any electronic or mechanical means, including information storage and retrieval systems, without permission in writing from the publisher, except by reviewers, who may quote brief passages in a review.

ISBN: 978-1-956736-49-6 (Paperback Edition)
ISBN: 978-1-956736-50-2 (Hardcover Edition)
ISBN: 978-1-956736-48-9 (E-book Edition)

Library of Congress Control Number: 2021920405

Book Ordering Information

Phone Number: 315 288-7939 ext. 1000 or 347-901-4920
Email: info@globalsummithouse.com
Global Summit House
www.globalsummithouse.com

Printed in the United States of America

Dedication

This book is dedicated to the millions of people whose lives have been spoiled, disrupted, or ended by behavior driven by the addiction to alcoholic drink. It is my strong desire that the information in this Book will provide convincing evidence that excessive use of alcoholic drink is in no way whatsoever, clever, cute, manageable, or intelligent. On a more personal level, I also want to dedicate this particular book to our collective 8 children (Alicia, Angela, Robin, Marvin 3, Amber, John Paul, Carlene, and Lisa).

You all have become responsible honest, loving, and generous American citizens, setting your individual goals for your own very different careers, and owning your own businesses. You've actually reached those goals with gusto and success! Bravo! I know those were not easy tasks to achieve.

You all have done the above by the grace of God and with much less than a desirable amount of parenting from myself. My absence as a parent was due to my alcoholism and being in Vietnam.

I am so grateful to be in recovery so that I can now enjoy you and your children. Charline's inability was due to her often working two jobs while getting her education as well as her unhealthy choices in marriages along the way.

So, congratulations for surviving your childhood and actually thriving as adults, almost totally on your own! Charline and I are very proud of you all and are honored to be your parents, flawed as we are.

Contents

Dedication 5

Chapter 1   The Six Disciplines Of Sobriety 9

Chapter 2   The Crucial Character Of Abstinence 33

Chapter 3   The Author's Story 42

Chapter 4   Sobriety-Speak 50

Chapter 5   The God Of The Impossible 55

Chapter 6   The Purpose Of Life 61

Chapter One

THE SIX DISCIPLINES OF SOBRIETY

"You never fail until you stop trying." Albert Einstein

"Not everything that is faced can be changed, but nothing can be changed until it is faced." James Baldwin

"The time is always right to do the right thing." Martin Luther King, Jr.

"If you want love and abundance in your life, give it away." Mark Twain

THE SIX DISCIPLINES

I have been waking up very early for the past several days with intensive thoughts about what I wanted to call these ideas I have been led to call the six disciplines of sobriety, and how to explain them to you in this Chapter of this book. I believe the origin of these ideas has been Divine, and I need to say "Thank You, Jesus, "for the messages." Here is my best effort at passing the information along to you, my readers.

The concepts I am calling the six disciplines of Sobriety are these;

1. **Read...** A.A., The Big Book.

2. **Attend...** meetings, 30 in 30 days.

3. **Obtain...** a sponsor.

4. **Pray...** unceasingly for yourself and others.

5. **Abstain...** from drinking alcoholic drinks.

6. **Contribute...** by helping others working the 12 steps.

DISCIPLINE NUMBER 1
READ

"One glance at a book, and you hear the voice of another person, perhaps dead for 1000 years, to read is to voyage through time." Carl Sagan

"There is more treasure in books, than in all the pirate's loot on Treasure Island." Walt Disney

"Once you read a book you care about, part of it is always in you." Louis L'Amour

"Think before you speak and read before you think." Fran Leibowitz

Alcoholics often end meetings in a tight circle reciting this slogan, "It works if you work it." In this chapter I am identifying six disciplines I believe are crucial to the success of working a program where the desired outcome is recovery, sobriety. It is no coincidence that the very first discipline on my list is expressed in the very simple, four-letter word, "read."

I strongly suggest that one of the first things a recovering alcoholic should do to begin "working" his or her program is to invest in what we could appropriately call the Bible for recovery, a Book called Alcoholics Anonymous, often referred to as "The Big Book." That Book was written by our founder, Bill Wilson, the man who launched this program which has delivered sanity to so many of us who were struggling with the chaotic insanity of addiction to alcohol. Thanks, Bill. I personally believe that much of what Bill said or wrote was inspired by God. Thanks, God.

I distinctly remember a lot about an episode of a TV Program I watched about 40 years ago. That is an amazing thing because you and I know that we sometimes have difficulty remembering what we watched on TV last night or even this morning. The episode was from a program such as "The Outer Limits," or "The Twilight Zone."

In the episode, in which I believe was portrayed by Burgess Meredith, the main character who passionately loved to read books. Unfortunately, he was terribly frustrated because the minutia of everyday life prevented him from his great love of reading. In the story, a catastrophic event ends the world, and the old man is the only living man left on Earth. He finds refuge in a huge Library, where he can happily end his life surrounded by thousands of books.

The story ends with a tragedy when the old man drops and accidently smashes his glasses. The story ends with the old man lamenting that he will live out his days surrounded by books he cannot read.

When I think about that program that has stayed with me for over 40 years I wonder and wish that I could leave the world with a passion for reading like the character in that story from a long, long time ago. I know and love someone who has that kind of passion for reading. In fact, I am married to one of the most avid readers I ever met. Charline has an IQ Score that qualifies her as a genius. I believe my lady's brilliance is revealed not only by a score on a test, but by her great passion for reading. She reads anything she can get into her hands. She reads trite novels and scholarly essays. My advice to anyone who would seek to improve themselves, their intelligence, their understanding of the world and the people in it, or simply come to a greater appreciation of life and its meaning is to read, to read and to keep reading.

More specifically, for our purposes on these pages we need to drink freely until we totally consume the written wisdom of our founder, Bill W. Thank God, he was not only a skilled orator, but he wrote better than most authors you will read today. His book, Alcoholics Anonymous, will get you started on your course of appreciation and understanding of why our program works, and of how you can work it. If you detest reading. then force yourself to read at least this one book, ALCOHOLICS ANONYMOUS, The Big Book.

I also believe it is very important for believers in the Lordship of Jesus Christ to become very familiar with His Book, The Holy Bible. No, Christ didn't write a word of the Bible, but he made sure His many secretaries got every word just as He intended for those words to be recorded. As the late Zig Ziglar used to say, "I believe the Bible from Genesis to Maps."Well said, Zig." And I agree with you; If the Bible says it, I believe it, and as far as I am concerned, that settles it.

The books of the Bible are not located in chronological order. To begin on the first page of the Bible, in Chapter one of the Book of Genesis, might lead to some confusion about the order of occurrences in the Bible. I heard Charles Stanley, the Pastor of the First Baptist Church of Atlanta, deliver some very good advice on where you might begin a program of daily Bible reading. I followed his advice and found the experience to be very empowering, and very easy to accomplish. Dr. Stanley suggested that you begin by reading the first eleven verses from the Book of Joshua, and that you read those verses every day for several days. I don't believe any of you will regret reading the first eleven verses of Joshua, every day for a week and a day, eight days. As you read these words remember that these are the instructions God gave to Joshua, thousands of years ago. Also keep in mind that God is giving you the very same guidance. Consider verse 9 where we read, "Have not I commanded thee? Be strong and of a good courage be not afraid, neither be thou dismayed, for the Lord God is with thee whithersoever thou goest." God does not tell us to do something unless he first equips us to follow His instruction. If God tells us to not be afraid nor to be not dismayed, then we are capable of precisely doing that. If God tells us He will never leave us, then He means that He will never leave us. I urge you to take comfort and strength from these few words.

When you are ready to make your commitment to daily Bible reading then I suggest that you begin by reading the Gospel of John. Then spend 15 or 30 minutes each day reading the word. If you are married, then reading together aloud is a great exercise. Think of what changes might occur in your home when God's holy words are heard, spoken by you and your spouse, in your home each day.

Finally, I suggest that you read the Book CODEPENDENT NO MORE, by Melody Beattie. You will benefit from learning more about the people who seem to be addicted to relationships with we addicts. My wife, Charline, told me that she has lost count of how many of these great little books she has given away to friends and asked clients to buy and read and reread.

DISCIPLINE NUMBER 2
ATTEND

In Alcoholics Anonymous it is almost always at our meetings where we meet the people who will prove vital to our recoveries, where we learn the ideas and strategies for moving from addiction into sobriety, and where we connect with the recovering addicts who will inspire and direct our own recoveries into sobriety, The Author

The core beating heartbeat of the 12-step recovery program from alcoholism is our meetings. Most of our meetings are conducted without a leader or recognized authority. The exception occurs when we have a rare speaker meeting and some recognized authority on recovery comes in and speaks. What makes our meetings work are the words of recovering alcoholics, who tell their stories or share things they are experiencing in their lives. Listening to the stories of others delivers three benefits. The first benefit is that by listening to others tell their stories we learn to construct and deliver our own stories. Secondly, we learn methods of coping with our addiction and of maintaining our own sobriety. The third benefit is less tangible and more spiritual in nature. Because of the third benefit each of us shares from the communal power of many thousands of recovering alcoholics around the world working our own programs to help us in our struggle to do exactly the same thing each of us is doing; working to maintain our sobriety and overcome our addiction to the life-sucking destruction of alcohol.

To describe the power of belonging to the international community of recovering alcoholics please allow me to slip into the vernacular of the hundreds of Wester Movies I watched with my Dad while I was a child back in Birmingham, Alabama. On Saturday evenings Dad and I would walk a couple of miles to watch our heroes with names like Whip Wilson, Red Ryder, and Lil Beaver, and Hopalong Cassidy. Over the past few decades, I have seen many miracles and a few disastrous failures come out of the International Fellowship we call Alcoholics Anonymous. I have come to think of the thousands of recovering alcoholics as the Sheriff's posse.

Those posses, in those old movies, were made up of either a few friends of the sheriff or of dozens of good men, willing to be temporarily deputized and to ride like thunder with a posse of similarly deputized men of the old West. Those deputies were good and unselfish men, willing to expose themselves to whatever cruelty the enemy had to throw at them, simply because they were the good-guys, and had made a commitment to do whatever it took to make the right thing happen.

The many thousands of recovering alcoholics are one gigantic posse, each of us determined to see ourselves recover and learn the skills required to live the rest of our lives alcohol-free. Every one of we former drunks is all-in, 120 per cent dedicated to our own recovery and to yours. That results in a great Cloud - bank of cosmic energy, a humongous force of good and righteous power, the power of each of us. we recovering alcoholics, pulling for you to succeed, to win, to come out sober and free from this twisted and atrocious addiction each of us does battle with every day of our lives.

Think for a minute about what that posse must look like when they are riding like an army of lunatics to your rescue. Picture them, ten and twenty riders deep, spread out over a mile across the prairie. Think about the great cloud of dust being kicked up by that wildly assorted stampede of horses. Picture the great Palominos, the Appaloosas, the Paint Ponies, and the grand Stallions. Every last one of those horses and every last rider is coming hard and fast, determined to witness your rescue, your sobriety, your freedom from the serpentine clutches of addiction. That, dear reader, is your posse, as dedicated to your cause as you yourself are dedicated. That, dear reader, is the sheer and awesome power of every recovering addict to alcohol in the world, pulling for you and for your ultimate victory. So go ahead and claim the inevitable victory that is yours. Lay a hard and unbreakable claim on your own sobriety. Now, pay close attention. Listen and hear. That rumbling in the distance, that shaking of the very ground beneath your feet. That. ladies and gentleman, is power, the unlimited power of numbers, or your posse, of the men and women who are totally fed up with the lies about the power of our addiction. They are your rescuers. They are your posse. Greet them. Embrace them.

Now, pick a good and strong steed. Saddle up. and mount up. Join us and let's end this ridiculous nonsense about an unbeatable addiction. Welcome to the posse, partner. Welcome, and may your trail be smooth and steady. Welcome to your own sanity. That town up ahead; we call it sobriety. Welcome, we've all been waiting for you. Welcome, home.

DISCIPLINE NUMBER 3
OBTAIN

"Everyone you meet knows something you don't." Bill Nye

"Life is beautiful not because of the things we do. Life is beautiful because of the people we meet." Simon Sinek

"You can make more friends in two months by becoming interested in other people, than you could make in two years by trying to make other people interested in you." Dale Carnegie

"Encourage everyone you meet with a smile or compliment. Make them feel better after they leave your presence, and they will be glad to see you coming." Joyce Meyer

You are assigned a vital quest as you begin to attend meetings. There is one particular tool you absolutely must have to complete your search for sobriety. You cannot do this alone. You need a helper and an authority to guide you through your mission. We call those men and women, who serve as our guides, sponsors. The sooner you locate and form a working relationship with someone willing to serve as your sponsor, the better. One of those old drunks has been waiting for you, searching for you, and looking forward to helping you negotiate the complicated and often twisted trail to sobriety.

When you find a sponsor with from two to five years sobriety, who is willing to stand by you as you become sober, you are truly blessed. They've "been there and done that" and will hold your feet to the fire when necessary to help keep you on the right track. Get ready for total honesty to your questions, with their observations and suggestions.

I used to love to drive long distances, alone at night, listening to the radio. One of my favorite people to listen to was Ed Doremus. One night I was driving just East of Houston, Texas when I heard Mr. Doremus recite a very brief poem. That poem sounded so important to me that I decided to recite it aloud many times, and to make those few words my own. The words were.

A bell is not a bell till you ring it, A song is not a song till you sing it,

Love was not put in your heart to stay, Because love isn't love till you give it away."

"Wow," I said to myself as I thought about those words. In these few paragraphs. I want to tell you a little bit of what I know and understand about sponsorship in Alcoholics Anonymous. As I've already stated, we don't have recognized leaders or authorities in Alcoholics Anonymous. Anyone, who has any slight bit of recovery becomes one of our authorities, because he or she has at least learned something about recovery, because he or she has lived it. The man or woman who has maintained even a few hours of sobriety, knows at least some small bit about the science or art of recovery from Alcoholism. That person is welcomed and encouraged to share whatever he or she has learned about sobriety. Like "Love" in the poem I heard from Ed Doremus, "Love only becomes love when it is given away." We recovering alcoholics believe knowledge only becomes knowledge when it is given away. So, the person who volunteers to speak at an Alcoholics Anonymous Meeting immediately becomes one of our recognized "Experts" on the subject of recovery. We recognize those people as experts because they were willing to share their well-earned wisdom with us.

I recently wrote that we might think of those people seated around us at our meetings as our posse. Here is another name for them; we could accurately call them "givers' because they freely give, at any opportunity, the wisdom which they are absolutely certain has worked for them. They know what the true value of their wisdom is because they sit in a room with you, sober and sane. Their truth is one of the most valuable things they have ever owned, and they casually and freely give it to whosoever might use it in his or her own recovery.

I have mentioned two sources of wisdom we can all use at Alcoholics Anonymous Meetings; we can ask our sponsors, or we can listen to the wisdom communicated by the drunks sitting next to you or across the room from you. Please understand that I use the term "drunks" referring to myself and others with the utmost admiration and respect. We "drunks" have done our own deadly combat with addiction, and somehow emerged victorious enough to attend meetings, and share our knowledge of something that worked for us in obtaining sobriety. Please accept the gratitude of a fellow drunk.

In selecting a sponsor, it's always best to find someone who is obviously working his or her own program. You can easily discern this by noting whether or not the person you are watching is working his or her own program. Clue number one is answered by this question, Is the person attending meetings? If out of the last ten meetings you attended was that person in attendance at eight of them? The next question is, are they making significant contributions at the meetings? If you are delaying asking someone to sponsor you because you are shy or afraid of rejection then get over that right now, this very minute. This is too important for you to delay because you don't have the gumption to walk up to someone and ask, "Will you be my sponsor?" Getting a sponsor is one of the very essential building blocks of success in the Alcoholics Anonymous program. Don't you dare delay it or put it off another day!

Yes, it takes a bit of grit, but do it anyway, and make sure you do it at the very next meeting you attend. This is just too important to put off for another day. This is your day to ask for a sponsor, so either do it, or just give up, and keep on drinking. It's that important. Please, stop making silly excuses and do what you know needs to be done this very day. Good luck, God bless you and your effort to achieve and maintain sobriety. You can do this. Just walk up to the person who God has led you to ask, say," Hello," and then say these words, "Will you be my sponsor?" The very worst thing that can happen is that the person you ask, says, "No." That won't kill you. Then look again, find another person you believe you can work with, and ask them. If someone said they would not sponsor you, that is because that person is not the one God picked out for you. Just keep looking. This is crucial to you and your sobriety. Please. do this today.

DISCIPLINE NUMBER 4
PRAY

"Is prayer your steering wheel or your spare tire." Corrie Ten Boom

"Prayer is a way of life, not just for use in case of emergencies. Make it a habit and when the need arises you will be in practice." Billy Graham

"Our prayers may be awkward; our attempts may be feeble. But since the power of prayer is in the One who hears it not the one who says it, our prayer can make a difference." Max Lucado

Travel back in time with me, now, way back to the 1940's, back to the day of Western MOVIES and TV Heroes. Almost all of those characters had a famous sidekick, someone the Directors had added for comic relief, a partner, who was not in every scene but was never far removed from the main cowboy. Gene Autry had Pat Buttram, Roy Rogers had Pat Brady, Hopalong Cassidy was around for many years and had several sidekicks, but none more famous than George "Gaby" Hayes, The Cisco Kid had Pancho, and Red Ryder had a young Indian Boy, Lil Beaver. Those "sidekicks" were always there, just out of sight, but they were there to help our heroes, to add a bit of humor, or, if needed, the firepower of an extra gun.

Up until the time he died, in his 80's, Pat Buttram met a couple of times each week for lunch with his old Movie partner, Gene Autry. Old friendships sometimes maintain their passion and importance over an entire lifetime. No relationship could possibly be as close as the one that God wants to form with you. I believe that some of the strongest and most significant words in the entire Bible are contained in the several variations of the verse where God All Mighty makes a promise and a divine guarantee that He will never leave nor forsake us. Here are a few examples of those verses.

In Deuteronomy 31:6. We read, "Be strong and of a good courage, fear not, nor be afraid of them: for the Lord thy God, He it is that goeth forth with thee, He will not fail thee nor forsake thee." Then in Genesis 28:15, we read, "And behold I am with thee, and will keep thee in all places wither thou goest and will bring thee again into this land: for I will not leave thee until I have done that which I have spoken to thee of." God obviously wanted us to know and appreciate that He was our constant companion, and that is the reason we find His promise of that companionship mentioned so many times in the Bible. In Joshua 1:9 we find these words, "Have not I commanded thee? Be strong and of a good courage; Be not afraid, neither be thou dismayed: For the Lord thy God is with thee withersoever thou goest. "

Paul exercised an extraordinarily highly developed skill in capturing the meanings in his writings with only a single word or two. We find a great example of that when Paul writes of how we should pray, in I Thesalonians, 5:17, Paul wrote, "Pray without ceasing." [Other versions of the Bible express this idea with the single word, "unceasingly. "]

I used this brief example of how God answers prayer in a previous book, and I only repeat it here because it so vividly illustrates how God can and does answer prayers. During the Yom Kippur War an Israeli Infantry patrol wandered one night into an enemy mine field. Suddenly one of the soldiers began to pray aloud. The Israelis were on their bellies, probing for the hidden mines with their knives and bayonets. Very quickly, after the one soldier began to pray aloud, a fierce and unusual wind began to blow across the mine field. Quickly, the wind blew away the dirt and sand concealing the mines. With the mines now clearly visible the men in the Israeli Patrol simply stood up and carefully walked around the mines, and out of the minefield to safety. At the very precise time when every soldier in that enemy minefield must have felt that God had left them, the truth was that God was there, and He proved His presence by saving that patrol.

We know, by God's own word, that He will never leave us. We know that we can communicate with Him at any instant, and we know that He is famous for answering prayers. I do not want to forget to ask for the mercy of God, every time I step down into an automobile; asking God to guard and protect the vehicle, it's driver and all the other vehicles around us. God has many promises in His book and He is a promise keeper!

So, go ahead. Pray unceasingly. Give it a try and see what a difference it makes in your life. Remember that He will give one of three answers; "yes, no or maybe later" and that His timing is always perfect.

DISCIPLINE NUMBER 5
ABSTAIN

"Drunkenness is nothing but temporary madness." Seneca

"Always do sober what you said you'd do drunk." Ernest Hemingway

"The day I became free of alcohol was the day I fully understood and embraced he truth that I would not be giving anything up by not drinking." Liz Hemingway

Much has been reported on the differences between a person who drinks too much, and a real-deal, diagnosable alcoholic. They are a different breed of cat. The cure to their problems, however, is identical. To obtain recovery-sobriety-it always requires that the person suffering from a problem with alcohol, launch a lifetime program of abstinence from any and all alcoholic drinking. Regardless of how severe the problem with drinking alcohol might be, the solution always begins when the drinking person makes a rock-solid decision to abstain from drinking for every day for the rest of their life, starting with one day at a time. That is all very simple…you stop drinking to begin your recovery and your new life of sobriety. My advice therefore is this- don't worry yourself with the severity of your alcoholic condition, but rather focus on your plan for staying sober for the rest of your life.

When that plan for abstinence becomes an integral part of who you are-one of the essentials of life that make you who you are, then you begin to embrace and to truly own your sobriety. All you have to do is the next right thing, simple but not necessarily easy.

The formula for escaping the addiction to alcohol and finding peace in sobriety is extremely simple; one moves from addiction to sobriety by abstaining from any alcoholic drink for the remainder of his or her lifetime. Some other addictions require a far more complicated termination. Compulsive overeaters or sex addicts for example, cannot simply abstain from eating or having sex forever. They must learn to eat with a complex list of rules. Compulsive shoppers can't simply stop shopping, but they must self-impose a set of complex rules on themselves that delivers their sanity and recovery.

The alcoholic almost always brings forward, from his or her addiction, certain dysfunctional and destructive behaviors, such as the blatant dishonesty they employed to maintain their addictions. Often those problems can be addressed, after the alcoholic stops drinking, by working with their sponsors and or by working the remainder of the 12 steps. Completion of a 12-step program should prove to be both therapeutic and life-changing. Sometimes even after completion of a 12-step program, additional therapy with a qualified therapist might be required to correct certain character flaws and problems.

I will focus now on the most obvious problem for the alcoholic, the problem of drinking alcohol. Until the addict completely stops drinking, nothing good or therapeutic can occur. Launching your own program of a lifetime of abstinence is your gateway to sanity, and your launching pad to sobriety. Volumes have been written about abstinence from alcohol, but I want to address the perfect time for you to launch your program. That time is this very day; you can begin your lifetime abstinence program today.

You might not survive one more bout of intoxication. Think about it. Getting drunk can, and often does, literally kill the drunk or someone else. You cannot afford the dangerous effects of one more day of being a drunk. So, whatever "reason" you have been using to delay your S-Day, or Sobriety Day, it is not a good reason and unworthy of you. Let it go and make a decision. Tell yourself, "This is my day, the day I stop drinking for the rest of my life. There can't be a sane and rational reason to put it off for one more day. This is it. Simply tell yourself, "This is my day."

Illusive Sobriety

Now, call the people you love, the members of your family and your best friend, and say this, "Today is my day, the day I stop drinking forever. I want you to go to supper with me to celebrate. Make sure to go someplace where alcohol isn't served. Go ahead, call your mom and dad, your best friends and make it official. Share the good news that you are now, and for the rest of your life, alcohol-free, starting today.

I'm going to ask you a question, but before I do that, I want to predict that you don't have a real or reliable answer to the question. The question is this; Do you have a real and reliable reason why you should delay launching your lifetime sobriety program one more day? I don't believe that question has a real or reliable answer. The best time for you to begin your program of sobriety through abstinence from alcohol is this very day, today, the first day of the rest of your life of sobriety. Think about it. Millions of us have been successful at with this grand freedom of life we call sobriety. If we can do it, then so can you.

I have been asked recently what I thought about the idea of abstaining from alcohol for 30 days, during the Month of January. That, dear readers is one of the most ridiculous and downright stupid ideas I ever heard. The goal of an addict, working a program in Alcoholics Anonymous, has never, ever been to remain sober for a month. Here is an undeniable fact; If you can remain sober, through abstinence from alcohol for 30 days, then you can remain sober for 30 years, or for the rest of your natural life. What pinhead decided to teach people to remain sober for 30 days instead of for a lifetime? If your goal is only 30 days of sobriety, guess what you are going to be concentrating on during that month. The answer is you are going to spend most of your waking moments thinking about the drink that awaits you at the end of your 30-day trial.

Think about that simple phrase you have heard dozens of times at meetings; "one day at a time." That is precisely how we do it, ladies, and gentlemen. We master sobriety by getting sober and by staying that way today, tomorrow and the day after that, for as long as we live. In other words, we cling to our precious sobriety, one day at a time, for the rest of our lives. I have stayed sober, one day at a time, for 33 years. Believe it or not, I am still severely tempted by the exact same lies that kept my addiction alive for almost 40 years, such as the lie that one drink would taste so good, that it couldn't hurt me and I could simply have that one drink, and that would be the end of it. What a boatload of bull that is. You know it, and so do I. The truth is this; I can't drink, and I have proved that to myself and others. All the lies will never change the fact that I cannot drink. So, I cling, ever so tenaciously, to my sobriety, and I do it one day at a time, because that, boys, and girls, is the very best I can do.

DISCIPLINE NUMBER 6
CONTRIBUTION

"We make a living by what we get, but we make a life by what we give." Winston Churchill

"Only those who have learned the power of complete and selfless contribution experience life's deepest joy, true fulfillment." Tony Robbins

"We ourselves feel that we are just a drop in the ocean. But the ocean would be less because of that missing drop." Mother Teresa

Steven Covey said. "Life is not about accumulation. It is about contribution." Wherever you are attending Alcoholics Anonymous Meetings, there is probably a small group of recovering men and/or women who frequently make intelligent and relevant contributions to what is being said. Those people sound intelligent because they have earned that intelligence though their successes in working their way through the process of recovery. Recovery from addiction does not happen instantly; it is a process that can, and often does, take years, and often am entire lifetime to execute. People with significant time in recovery have lived through what is often the sheer terror of recovery. They have paid a price, often, a very costly price, for their recovery.

Many recovering alcoholics think of contributing back to the program that helped them to restore sanity to their lives as their "payback time," a time to pay back for the life-restoring dose of sanity they once received from Alcoholics Anonymous. Previous strangers, with no obvious reason to help others, worked to help them restore sanity to their often-miserable lives. No member of Alcoholics Anonymous should ever ask for compensation for helping other alcoholics. We help each other simply because that is one of the founding underpinnings that was used to launch our group, and because it is simply the right thing to do. We are a society of nobody's. thriving and surviving because we embrace the noble pursuit of helping each other to make it through this monstrosity we call addiction. We help each other because a stranger once helped us, and we still realize and appreciate the invaluable worth of a helping hand.

The main things to take away from chapter 1 are.

Marvin Sprouse

This Page Is Provided For Notes On Chapter One.

Chapter Two

THE CRUCIAL CHARACTER OF ABSTINENCE

A FRIEND OF BILLS "Then you will know what it means to give of yourself that others may survive and rediscover life. You will learn the full meaning of "Love thy neighbor as thyself." This quotation is from The Big Book, page 153 written primarily by Bill Wilson, the acknowledged founder of Alcoholics Anonymous. The last five words of the quotation are from The Bible, Matthew 22:39.

"The idea that somehow, someday he will control and enjoy his drinking is the great obsession of every abnormal drinker." Bill Wilson, The Big Book

Why People Drink Alcohol

"Because alcohol is encouraged by our culture, we get the idea that it isn't dangerous. However, it is the most potent and most toxic of the legal psychoactive drugs. "Beverly A. Potter and Sebastian Orfali

"Talking to a drunk person is like talking to an extremely happy, severely brain-damaged-3- year-old." John Green

"A man wo drinks too much is still the same man as he was sober. An alcoholic, a real alcoholic, is not the same man at all. You can't predict anything about him for sure except he will be someone you never met before." Raymond Chandler

People drink alcohol, not because they become addicted to

its taste in certain drinks, but because of the feelings they get from drinking to intoxication. Under the influence of alcohol some people are able to do things they believe they could not accomplish without an infusion of alcohol, sometimes referred to as "liquid courage."

In Susan Cheever's book, MY NAME IS BILL, I read that Bill Wilson was attending a fancy ball, where waiters he described as "butlers" were walking around, carrying trays of cocktails, free to the guests at the event. Bill Wilson reported that he was determined not to drink alcohol, because of the chaos it had brought to several members of his family. However, with an attractive woman by his side, and when he was offered the complimentary drinks, he reported that he just didn't know how to refuse the drinks. Of course, you and I know that he could have saved himself years of grief with the three simple words, "No, thank you,"

Bill Wilson then said that he surprised himself after three or four drinks, insomuch as he was speaking to several groups of people with eloquence and humor, and that they appeared to appreciate all that he had to say. Do you find that astonishing? Remember, that after he stopped drinking, Mr. Wilson was one of the premiere speakers in our Country. He was vigorously sought after as a speaker, and captivated audiences with the things he said. As so often happens in the use of alcohol, the alcoholic believes they lack certain skills, and can only activate those particular skills through the use of alcohol. Actually, they often already have a mastery of the skills they believe can only be accessed under the influence of alcohol. In the case of Bill Wilson, he actually believed that he could be transformed into a talented and effective speaker only through partial intoxication. Of course, that is not true, and all partial intoxication does for a speaker is to cause him or her to slur his or her words, and to be left, after returning to sobriety, with a hazy memory of what was said and of how it was actually received.

How Some People Stop Drinking

Alcohol has often been called "liquid courage" because many people consume alcohol, believing that it will somehow bolster up their resolve, and bring them the courage they believe they lack to perform certain tasks at a perceived "higher" level of competence than they believe they are capable of delivering without alcohol. More often than not, the people who doubt their own natural abilities to deliver a performance with a high degree of competence, are denying the God-given skill levels they already own. They look to alcohol to increase the level of their performance. Actually, alcohol fails miserably as a performance enhancing elixir. To begin with, there is absolutely no existing method for predicting an appropriate dosage of alcohol, to accomplish any particular task. The eleven ounces of Bourbon you used to deliver a flawless briefing this afternoon could very well leave you mumbling and slurring your words tomorrow.

When we look for alcohol to supply what we perceive as a deficit of personal courage, that search actually violates the instruction which was specifically delivered to each of us by God All-Mighty. In Joshua 1:9, God is speaking not only with His servant, Joshua, but directly with each of us, when He said, "Have not I commanded thee? Be strong and of a good courage: be not afraid, neither be thou dismayed: for the Lord God is with thee, withersoever thou goest." Please note that God is neither suggesting nor implying that we should always. and in all situations move fearlessly through this journey we call life and count on Him to guide and to protect us on each step of our adventure. He is emphatically commanding us to not entertain fear or dismay. Commanding us, readers. Please keep in mind, God never commands us to do anything we are not equipped to accomplish. God thoroughly equips to deal with each episode of life with more than adequate courage and confidence.

When a person is tempted by alcohol, at least temporarily

believing that the alcohol in a drink actually does supply liquid courage, we can find refuge from that nonsensical belief in the promise God made that He will never leave nor forsake us. Never means never when God promises it to any or to all of us. The very best reason I can imagine to not drink or to stop drinking alcohol, is because its promises of alcohol are all false and phonies, AND because each of us has the irrefutable and bullet-proof power of God's own promise that He will never leave nor forsake us. To choose for even one more drink to accept the lie of any positive power hiding out in a bottle of alcohol, and to reject a direct and emphatic promise from God is only a silly lie.

Belief in the restorative power of alcohol is about 40,000 leagues beneath stupid. Think about it and sober up. Then move forward with your life, "being of a good courage." Don't take my word for it after - all, God said it-not me.

THE MARSHMALLOW TESTS

In 1972, at Stanford University, Psychologist Walter Michael conducted the first of a series of tests that would come to be known as "The Marshmallow Tests." The subjects of those tests were three- to five-year-old children.

Each child was ushered into a room and seated at a table. On each table was a plate containing a single marshmallow. Each child was told by the proctor that he or she would leave the room and return in about 15 minutes. Each child was also told that if they did not eat the marshmallow in front of them, they would be rewarded with an additional marshmallow. The children were also told that if they decided to eat the marshmallow, they could ring a bell and the proctor would return.

Some of the behavior exhibited by the children who refrained from eating the marshmallows proved very interesting to the observers. Some of the children distracted themselves from the marshmallows by going to a remote place in the room and conducting vigorous exercise, such as running in place.

Many years after the original studies were conducted, it was observed that those who ate their original marshmallows tended to have less satisfactory life outcomes than the subjects who managed to abstain from eating their marshmallows. More specifically, the studies appeared to help in identifying those who had strengths and those who had diminished skills in delayed gratification.

When the results of the studies were published many parents attempted to replicate the studies in their own homes with their own children. One of those home-based-studies revealed a little girl who took her marshmallow apart, ate the gooey center of it, and then resealed the marshmallow, attempting to conceal the fact that she had actually eaten part of the marshmallow.

When I heard about the child who tried to conceal the fact that she had eaten the best part of her marshmallow, my mind immediately flashed to the idea that that child's behavior sounded much like the actions of an adult addict. Part of the disease of addiction is our dishonesty concerning our disease. Believe this, dear readers. dishonesty related to our disease is an integral part of the disease of addiction. Some of the most frequently used lies we tell ourselves are, "I can handle just this one drink," or "Just this one time it will be all right and it won't hurt me."

We have just entered into the area we addicts know as Magical Thinking. Please give consideration to this definition. Magical Thinking occurs when an addict knows that all the facts support an outcome other than the one, he anticipates, BUT because of Magical thinking, the addict is convinced that his action will result in the outcome he wants to occur. Magical thinking requires the addict to believe he can actually "will" a particular outcome into existence. Dear reader, it doesn't work that way, not ever. We do indeed get precisely what we deserve.

During my prayer time this morning I asked God to tell me how to explain the importance of abstinence to you. This is what he told me to tell you. Imagine that you are a parent watching your children. You watch your son walk up to your daughter, and hit her really hard with his fist, in her face. You have to intervene. Now, imagine that you tell your son, "Don't hit her quite that hard next time." That would be ridiculous. Of course, what you must communicate is, "Never, ever, under any circumstance, ever hit your sister again. Not ever."

It would be absurd for you to tell your son how to hit his sister next time, because that behavior is never, ever acceptable. There are some things that are just not acceptable, not ever, and hitting one's sister sure as lightening is one of those things you can never, ever tolerate. Another thing you can never allow again is for you to take a drink, not even a tiny sip of anything containing alcohol.

For you, drinking anything containing alcohol just does not fit. It cannot be part of your life, so don't do it. You must have 100 per cent abstinence. No exceptions. It is essential to your very life. No exceptions, total abstinence, and that is that.

I will close this Chapter by telling you how I stopped 50 years of hard drinking 33 years ago. I walked into a room, and I saw Charline, for the first time. I told myself immediately, "If that beautiful woman is not married, I will get her to marry me." When I asked Charline to marry me a few months later, she replied, "I will, if you quit drinking." I shot back at her, with my truth. I said, "I just did." That, dear reader, is how I stopped drinking, and how I have remained sober for 33 years. Being married to the most beautiful woman I ever saw is far better than the best drink I ever had. As I like to say, "That's my story, and I'm sticking to it."

Marvin Sprouse

The main points of chapter 2 are.

This Page Is Provided For Notes On Chapter Two

Chapter Three

THE AUTHOR'S STORY

I always prided myself as being the "class clown." People often told me that people weren't laughing with me but at me. I never understood the difference between the two. I always thought of myself as being an entertainer. I would take my guitar to school and team up with one of the cheerleaders to sing at assemblies. One of my favorite songs to sing was. "I'M IN THE JAILHOUSE NOW." If I couldn't sing at assemblies I would stage my own antics, such as one time after school, I ran through the sprinklers on a Church lawn across the street from our school, and then ran over and planted a big kiss on one of the cheerleaders who was practicing on the sidewalk in front of the church.

The first time I got drunk was at a wedding. We lived in a modest house a half block away from Ensley Park, a big and beautiful green park with a huge swimming pool and a community center where we attended Scout Meetings and played basketball. Partially because my mother kept her house immaculately maintained and because we were so close to the park, several people persuaded Mom to allow their children to be married in our home. The refreshments for those weddings always included copious amounts of wine and other alcoholic drinks. At those weddings I found I could drink enough to feel really great about acting stupid and making my relatives laugh. Life was good, really good.

When I graduated from high school, I went off to attend college at Memphis State, where I had been given a football scholarship. During one of the practice sessions, I was injured by a deep cut across my chin. The coaches offered to allow me to keep my scholarship if I would become the team's laundry boy. In my young and vain way of thinking I thought of myself as much better than serving as a laundry boy. I left Memphis State and joined the Army for six months. I fell in love with soldiering, and immediately realized one thing; that the way to serve in the Military was as an officer. I attended a Military School in Alabama, The Marion Military Institute, where I could also indulge another of my great loves, playing Football, on Marion's Junior College team. I earned a small, partial scholarship and took out a hefty College Loan to pay for attending college.

My drinking continued, and whenever I could, I would sneak off and go on a rowdy bender, chug-a-lugging a small ocean of beer. I often went to movies in Marion, and usually took along one of two beautiful young girls who were attending a nearby Girl's School, Judson College. In one of the most humiliating events of my entire life, two of the brothers of the girls I had been dating came and asked me to not date their sisters. I had never done anything to disrespect either of those girls, but my reputation as a drunk persuaded those two young men to do what they could to protect their sisters from me.

During my sophomore year I made a phone call and set up an interview with a dear friend, who was a year ahead of me in college, Chris Vaughn, with the head coach of the football team at a small local college in Birmingham, Howard College. Soon after that interview Howard College released their name to another school known as Howard College, and the Birmingham school became Samford College. The coach at Samford met with Chris, along with my Dad and I, on a summer afternoon. We sat on the steps at Samford, and listened to the soon to be famous coach, Bobby Bowden. The coach then spoke to me. He said, "Marvin, while I was watching films of Chris, I was also impressed watching you play. Would you like to join Chris, and play football here at Howard?"

That, obviously, was a golden opportunity, being offered

to me by one of the greatest football coaches of all time. Keep in mind, that Bobby Bowden was also known as a Christian gentleman, with high moral standards. The next year he would leave Howard College and begin his reign of excellence at Florida State University. I quickly responded to Coach Bowden with my idiotic response, "No thank you, coach." I turned down the coach's offer of a scholarship for one imbecilic reason. I wanted to attend college out of Birmingham and the supervision of my parents. I wanted to continue with my wild and rowdy bouts of drunkenness without the scrutiny of my parents. I can think clearly now, and I realize that playing for Coach Bowden would probably have required me to grow up and knock off the insanity of drunken behavior, or misbehavior, that had sort of become my calling card.

After College I was off to join the Army, as a Second Lieutenant. The military was a perfect place for a drunk who wanted to remain addicted to alcohol. We celebrated such events as my graduation from Airborne and Ranger Schools with bouts of noisy and boisterous drinking. I spent two tours in Viet Nam with uncountable bouts of drinking and of getting "knee-walking drunk.".

Later, I was promoted to Captain, and, on one occasion, I attended an intelligence Conference in Germany. One night, during that conference, I wound up in a bar, drunkenly talking to an Irish Soldier, who turned out to be one of my distant cousins from County Cork in Ireland. After a couple of beers, the Irishman and I decided to go outside and fight. {That makes no sense at all, dear reader, but it is precisely the sort of thing that Irish drunks in bars do.] There was not enough space for a proper fight in front of the bar, so the Irishman and I got into my car and drove half a block to a vacant lot for our fight.

Suddenly, I was arrested by the German Police, and charged with drunk driving. A Drunk-Driving Charge for an officer, stationed in Europe, is virtually the end of his career. He is sent

Illusive Sobriety

home and discharged, and his time of service in the military is ended.

I waited anxiously for the paperwork to get through the system so I could be confronted with my drunken misbehavior. Notification final caught up with me while I was at home eating lunch and, of course, drinking, on a Thanksgiving Day. I received a phone call at my home requesting me to come into the Army Headquarters Building to accept a phone call. The call was from an Army Major at an Army Headquarters over our own Unit. The Major told me that he had reviewed the record of my arret for drunk driving, and that he did not want to see the Army lose an officer over the incident, and that he was "losing" the file and all records of my arrest.

I was very excited about receiving a rescue from the ruining of my Army career, I rushed home for a celebration. The celebration, of course involved getting drunk on the wine and Bourbon I had in store at my home.

After about 40 years of hard drinking, and of barely getting by with my life. I met Charline, the most beautiful woman I ever saw. Charline was so incredibly beautiful that I knew immediately, when I first saw her, that she was the girl I wanted to marry and to be with for the rest of my life. Incredibly, as soon as I got to know Charline, I found that she was as kind, generous and giving as she was beautiful. I intelligently asked that beautiful lady to marry me, and she told me she would if I quit drinking. That was a no-brainer. Drinking had only caused me trouble, and to give it up for life, AND to get Charline as a bonus, didn't require a lot of thinking. When Charline asked if I would quit drinking, I immediately said goodbye to getting drunk and the horrible hangovers and I answered, "I just did" {quit drinking.}

Soon after we were married, Charline suggested that I attend some meetings of Alcoholics Anonymous. She had been counseling addicts for years and knew I would need help maintaining my sobriety. The first time I went to a meeting I remember driving around the block where the meeting was being held, four times before I finally parked and went inside. After I found the room where the AA Meetings were being held, it took me another six months before I could actually say the words, "I'm Marvin, and I'm an alcoholic." That was an amazing thing. I was attending a meeting in a room surrounded by people who all confessed of being alcoholics, and I was terrorized to have them find out that I was actually one of them; a guy who had experienced trouble with addiction to alcohol.

I attended 12 step meetings for a couple of years, both for Alcoholic Anonymous and for Compulsive Overeaters. I credit my experiences in those programs as the prime movers in restoring sanity to my insane life.

I have heard men representing various religions say that 12 step programs are dangerous and can come between a man and his relationship with God. The exact opposite of that happened to me. After working through the first three of the 12 steps, I discovered that working those steps had ignited in me a deep hunger for a closer and more passionate relationship with God. I attended a Church in Las Cruces, New Mexico, pastored by Jim Dixon, and Pastor Dixon taught me about the need to ask Jesus for salvation, and to come to a deeper and more meaningful relationship with Him. After leaving Las Cruces, and returning to my home in Texas, I met Pastor Jimmy Nelson, and joined the Church where he served as Pastor, Landmark Baptist Church in Fort Worth. There is a seminary attached to Landmark Baptist Church. While I attended that Seminary I earned three doctoral degrees, and later served as a professor, teaching classes on religious writing, and speaking. Charline also earned two Doctorates at that Seminary.

I left the Landmark Baptist Church after I came to believe in some doctrines that were contrary to many traditional Baptist beliefs, such as the Baptism of the Holy Ghost, man's ability to perform divine healing in the name of Jesus Christ, and other things such as speaking in tongues. I believe that working one's way through a 12-step program should always wind up in a logical position, closer to the truth of the significance that our God is alive, and rules today from his heavenly throne. I will always remain grateful to men such as pastor Jim Dixon, and Dr. Jimmy Nelson who labor daily in the pursuit of God's doctrinal truths.

Marvin Sprouse

The most important concepts in chapter 3 that are available to me to use immediately are.

Illusive Sobriety

This Page Is Provided For Notes On Chapter Three

Chapter Four

SOBRIETY-SPEAK

"Once you replace negative thoughts with positive ones, you start having positive results." Willie Nelson

"The positive thinker sees the invisible, feels the intangible, and achieves the impossible." Winston Churchill

"One small positive thought in the morning can change your whole day." Zig Ziglar

"You can't control the world, but when you control your thoughts, you bring order," Bernie Segal

"When the negative thoughts come-and they will, they come to all of us, it's not enough to just not dwell on it…you have to replace it with a positive thought." Joel Osteen

I believe the first five words of the Bible capture much of the essence and spirit of the entire Holy Bible. Those words are," In the beginning God created…" Create is defined as, "To make from nothing" and I believe God is the only one Who has ever done that. I heard one preacher describe creation this way. He said, "God stood on nothing, reached out into nowhere, gathered up a handful of nothing and spoke the universe into existence. "

Almost daily I am amused by people who make presentations to other people of awards for "creativity." I do not believe man has ever created anything. When a recording artist records a song, for example, it is never "created." It was written only after the artist had listened to hundreds of other songs, and it was written on a piece of paper containing musical staffs. In no way was it created or made from nothing. Consider the author of some great book. It was written only after the author had read hundreds, or possibly thousands of other books. Man conceives, erects, designs, or builds. God alone creates.

Notice specifically how God created all that was created. He spoke things into existence. When He spoke the words, for example, "Let there be light," then light immediately came into existence. At the instant when God said, "Let there be light," great galaxies appeared, complete with stars, suns, moons and with rotating and spinning planets, all moving in absolute and perfect harmony.

In what is certainly a power much weaker than God's power, man owns the ability to speak certain things into existence. Authors Richard Bandler and John Grinder have written about man's capability to bring things which do not exist into existence with their two Books, THE STRUCTURE OF MAGIC, Books 1 and 2. Man owns a remarkable and very powerful ability to speak life into things with his words.

Consider the alcoholic who is convinced that he or she has an "incurable disease." When that alcoholic speaks, with unshakable passion and conviction, those words, "Today is the day I quit drinking forever," then those simple words seal the deal, and the alcoholic is free from addiction. I am not talking about simply mumbling the words, but I am writing that when spoken with all you have going for you, then those words take on a "magical" or "Miraculous Power." If you believe this is a lot of nonsense, then you are absolutely correct. If, on the other hand, you believe these words just might work for you, then you also are absolutely correct. Here are a few affirmations you might want to speak over yourself and whatever limitation you might believe about yourself, and your ability to establish an unshakable ownership over your very own sobriety.

Today I stopped drinking alcohol, and I will embrace sobriety for as long as I live.

I used to drink alcohol, but I stopped doing that because it was too painful.

God is my own personal coach in my sobriety.

I maintain my sobriety, one day at a time, and can do that for as long as I live.

I simply let go of my addiction, and it no longer bothers me.

I'll close with these simple words, "Come on and own your sobriety. Talk it up."

Illusive Sobriety

The main things that I plan to use from chapter 4 are.

Marvin Sprouse

This Page Is Included For Notes On Chapter Four

Chapter Five

THE GOD OF THE IMPOSSIBLE

"Possible is impossible without change. so those who cannot change their minds cannot change anything." George Bernard Shaw

"Nothing is impossible. the word itself saying, "I'm possible." Audrey Hepburn

'I think that nothing is impossible when you want to fulfill a dream. A lot of people will tell you that you can't do it, that you don't have what it takes, but if it is in your heart, and you feel it, there is nothing that will stop you. It is like the sun-you can't block it. It will shine regardless of if that is what you want." Thalia

"It is difficult to say what is impossible, for the dream of yesterday is the hope of today, and the reality of tomorrow." Robert H Goddard

"The difference between the impossible and the possible lies within a man's determination." Tommy Lasorda

You might be one of the many hundreds of thousands of alcoholics who believe they are hopelessly addicted to drinking alcohol. Many are addicted without hope or any significant belief in their ability to become and to remain sober. Here, reader is the good news, the great news. We happen to serve an awesome God, who specializes in accomplishing the impossible. Not only did our God speak the entire Universe into existence, but He raised the dead, cured all kinds of diseases, drove out devils with the mere sound of His voice, caused the deaf to hear and the blind to see, and never, not a single time, ever, encountered anything He thought of as impossible.

Consider the miracle God effortlessly preformed when He parted the waters and saved His people from Pharoah's Army. History Books tell us that over a million Israeli slaves marched out of Egypt, during that great exodos. Imagine the size of that great Nation of people. For perspective consider that if the Dallas Cowboys Stadium, when packed, with every seat filled, holds 80,000 people, were emptied out and if everyone in that stadium was to go out and stand in a great empty field.

Then it would take 12 full stadiums of people to equal the size of the crowd that came marching out of Egypt, following an old man named Moses, who carried only his staff. Now, imagine that Nation of souls complimented by all sorts of livestock. There were thousands of chickens and pigs running in and out and around that mass of humanity. There were donkeys, mules and possibly a few horses. There were young children along with old men and women, all doing their very best to keep up with the swam of humanity as they walked out of Egypt. The closest things they carried to weapons were mere tools of farming, hoes, rakes, and ploughs.

Not long after the Nation of Israel walked out of their homeland, Pharoah had a drastic change of heart and mind. He probably reasoned that he was probably the most powerful Military Commander in the world, and that he had just given total freedom to the very people whose God had brought so many horrible and painful plagues upon his people. Furiously, he assembled his entire Army, fielding a force of soldiers equipped with swords and javelins, and riding in the most sophisticated chariots money could buy. Pharoah took his place front and center of that great force, and it must have sounded like a cataclysmic clap of thunder when all those chariots began roaring off in frenzied pursuit of over a million Jewish Slaves.

Keep in mind that almost every one of those Egyptian men-of-war had received a horrible visit the night before the exodus of over a million Jewish slaves, from The Angel of the Lord who came into their homes to deliver the most atrocious of all the plagues on Egypt, the killing of the family's firstborn. Certainly, each of those soldiers was driven by a ravenous bloodlust, to avenge themselves against those hated Jews. If they had been able to trap those Jewish Slaves, with their backs to the Red Sea, with no escape possible, history would have recorded that very day one of the most horrible massacres ever delivered on this Planet. The solution to the dilemma of the Jews was in the fact that they were called "My People" by the Supreme Ruler and Owner of the entire universe. Keep in mind that God does not tolerate the word "impossible" in His vocabulary.

When it appeared that all was lost and a bloody annihilation was inevitable, God showed Moses how to open up the equivalent of a Superhighway right through the deep waters of the Red Sea. Moses simply pointed his staff at the waters, and a great avenue was immediately opened in the waters. Close behind the escaping Jews was the entire Egyptian Army, led by Pharaoh in the lead chariot. When the Egyptians saw the miraculously constructed escape route they drove their horses, without a second's hesitation, in continued pursuit of the escaping slaves.

So far, I have devoted a few paragraphs to telling the remarkable story of creation, and these few paragraphs telling you about how God parted the waters of the Sea, to allow the safe escape of His People, the Jews. To know anything at all about the awesome God we serve we can never forget that our precious God lives completely without limitation. With our God, all things, absolutely all things, are possible.

If you are living and believing that recovery from addiction to alcohol is somehow impossible for you, then stop thinking that nonsense right now. Such thoughts are frivolous and unworthy of any person who has even a weak relationship with God All Mighty, the Creator and absolute Ruler of all that is or ever was. Your God simply does not believe in the impossible or entertain any concerns about things which some believe cannot exist, and neither should you. On the day you decided to make Jesus Christ the Lord of your life, you sailed out far beyond the world of impossibilities. Please, think about it. Do you believe, for an instant, that the God Who created the entire Universe with only a few of His spoken words that you could possibly get stuck on your belief that your addiction is incurable?

That is preposterous thinking. The God of all things miraculous is waiting patiently, right this second, for you to "Let us therefore come boldly unto the throne of grace, that we may obtain mercy, and obtain grace to help in time of need." ... Hebrews, 4:16, and simply speak these simple words, "Father, I need your help." So, go ahead and try it. I dare you.

Illusive Sobriety

The main points of chapter 5 that are relevant to me in improving my life are.

Marvin Sprouse

This Page Is Provided For Notes On Chapter Five

CHAPTER SIX

THE PURPOSE OF LIFE

"When you get a group of people that believe, are passionate, and committed to a single purpose, you better look out. Great things can happen." Dabo Sweeney

"I believe that God has put talent and ability on the inside of every one of us. When you believe in yourself, and you believe that you are a person of influence, and a person of purpose, I believe you can move out of any situation." Joel Osteen

"Work gives you meaning and purpose, and life is empty without it." Steven Hawking

While we, as a Nation, braced and attempted to prepare for the arrival of the Covid virus, we heard many reports concerning the physical and medical vulnerability of our older citizens. In one single report I heard that one of the leading causes of death among seniors was that "they wanted to die." I only heard that report one single time, probably because it was not a welcomed thought and most of us just didn't want to hear it.

I personally found the idea that many older Americans "wanted to die," to be very troubling. When I heard that I was approaching my 80th birthday, and I enjoyed life very much. I eagerly looked forward to every day and believed that I had a lot to live for, many reasons to continue living as long as I possibly could. It was during those days that I found a quotation from David Jeremiah, that both inspired and comforted me. He said, "A man of God. In the will of God, is immortal until the work is finished."

If a man with a purpose in life, that is pleasing to God will live until he completes that work, then that man lives with a great enthusiasm and an excitement for his life. Considering those words, gave me a boost to my enthusiasm to get up and out of bed each day and to continue writing what I believe are the exact words God wants me to write.

Sadly, many of our citizens believe that their purpose in life is to acquire money and the trappings of wealth. That is such a very limiting thought. I heard a story about Mother Teresa that gives me a clear insight of why man is not destined to work his hardest merely to accumulate stuff. A man had traveled a long way merely to meet Mother Teresa. When he finally did locate her, he found her in a filthy shack, sitting in the dirt, holding the head of a frail and dying older woman, in her lap, as she fed her spoons full of soup. The man said to Mother Teresa, "I wouldn't do that for a million dollars." Mother Teresa wisely replied, "Neither would I."

Don't make the mistake that "doing the will of God," requires your work to be assigned by a recognized church. When you fulfill God's instruction to "Love thy neighbor," you are in His will, doing His work by actually dispensing his love to one or more human beings, God's own people. Deliver free food, help non ambulatory people to move, or simply bring comfort to a lonely soul. All of those things are in the will of God.

Now, let's relate this back to our primary subject, beating addiction and finding recovery in sobriety. I realize that tragically for some of our friends who are still doing battle with their addiction to alcohol, finding a drink of alcohol has become their purpose in life. You are so much better and so much more than that. You deserve to replace your craving for a drink of alcohol with something more, something more worthy of who you are and what God intended for you to become. So, look around and find a person or group of people who have a need, and then do whatever you can to fill their need. Want to change your life, then change your focus. Concentrate not on what you want, but on what someone other than yourself, actually needs. You will really love the difference this will make in your life. I promise it's true.

This Page Is Provided For Notes On Chapter Six

Illusive Sobriety

The most important ideas in chapter 6 that I can apply to my life today are.

www.ingramcontent.com/pod-product-compliance
Lightning Source LLC
LaVergne TN
LVHW040201080526
838202LV00042B/3262